Westward Expansion

AMERICA'S PUSH TO THE PACIFIC

# THE MEXICAN-AMERICAN WAR



LAURA LORIA

Britannica Educational Publishing

IN ASSOCIATION WITH

ROSEN

EDUCATIONAL SERVICES

Published in 2018 by Britannica Educational Publishing (a trademark of Encyclopædia Britannica, Inc.) in association with The Rosen Publishing Group, Inc.
29 East 21st Street, New York, NY 10010



Distributed exclusively by Rosen Publishing.
To see additional Britannica Educational Publishing titles, go to rosenpublishing.com.

First Edition

**Britannica Educational Publishing**
J.E. Luebering: Executive Director, Core Editorial
Andrea R. Field: Managing Editor, Compton's by Britannica

**Rosen Publishing**
Heather Moore Niver: Editor and Photo Researcher
Nelson Sá: Art Director
Tahara Anderson: Designer
Cindy Reiman: Photography Manager

**Library of Congress Cataloging-in-Publication Data**

Names: Loria, Laura, author.
Title: The Mexican-American War / Laura Loria.
Description: New York : Britannica Educational Publishing, in Association with Rosen Educational Services, 2018 | Series: Westward expansion: America's push to the Pacific | Audience: Grades 5–8. | Includes bibliographical references and index.
Identifiers: LCCN 2017018665| ISBN 9781680487930 (library bound : alk. paper) | ISBN 9781680487923 (pbk.: alk. paper) | ISBN 9781538300145 (6 pack: alk. paper)
Subjects: LCSH: Mexican War, 1846–1848—Juvenile literature.
Classification: LCC E404 .L88 2018 | DDC 973.6/2—dc23
LC record available at https://lccn.loc.gov/2017018665

*Manufactured in the United States of America*

**Photo credits:** Cover, p. 32 DEA/G. Dagli Orti/De Agostini/Getty Images; p. 5 Encyclopædia Britannica, Inc.; p. 9 Pat Eyre/Alamy Stock Photo; p. 11 Library of Congress, Washington D.C. (reproduction no. LC-USZ62-21276); p. 13 Library of Congress, Washington, D.C. (Digital file no. cph 3g02133); p. 14 Universal Images Group/Getty Images; pp. 17, 27 Library of Congress, Washington, D.C.; p. 18 Art Collection 3/Alamy Stock Photo; p. 21 Printed Ephemera Collection; Portfolio 198, Folder 4—Rare Book and Special Collections/Library of Congress, Washington, D.C. (rbpe 19800400); pp. 22, 30 Hulton Archive/Archive Photos/Getty Images; p. 24 Universal History Archive/Universal Images Group/Getty Images; pp. 25, cover and interior pages (banner) Library of Congress Prints and Photograph Division; p. 29 Library of Congress, Washington, D.C. (cph 3b50618); p. 33 Library of Congress, Washington, D.C. (file no. LC-USZC2-1948); p. 34 M.Sobreira/Alamy Stock Photo; p. 37 Library of Congress/Corbis Historical/Getty Images; p. 39 Everett Collection Inc/Alamy Stock Photo; p. 41 Print Collector/Hulton Archive/Getty Images; p. 42 Bettmann/Getty Images.

# CONTENTS

# INTRODUCTION

In the early days of the United States, the nation was frequently engaged in conflict of one kind or another. There were wars to establish and defend America's independence, such as the American Revolution and the War of 1812. There were conflicts with Native Americans, a result of the country's desire to expand its territory. The Mexican-American War (1846–1848) was a conflict between neighbors. What began as a border dispute in Texas led to massive bloodshed for Mexico, huge land gains for the United States, and a damaged relationship between bordering nations.

Why did America's hunger for land require going to war? Part of the answer lies in the concept of Manifest Destiny. This was the nineteenth-century belief that it was America's divinely assigned mission to expand westward across North America and to spread democratic and Protestant ideals. John O'Sullivan, a journalist, coined the phrase in an 1845 newspaper

A dispute over the border of Texas led to war between the United States and Mexico in 1846. The Treaty of Guadalupe-Hidalgo, which ended the war in 1848, gave the United States a vast tract of Mexican territory extending to the Pacific Ocean.

editorial about the annexation of Texas, in which he spoke of America's "manifest destiny to overspread the continent allotted by Providence for the free development of our multiplying millions." The roots of the concept, however, can be traced to American and European writers of the colonial period and even earlier who professed the belief that the replacement of the pagan practices of American Indians in the West was no less than an ordination from God. The term was used as justification for the US acquisition of territory all the way to the Pacific Ocean.

Another motivation for the Mexican-American War was economic. The Mexican territories of New Mexico (which, at that time, included much of what is now the southwestern United States) and, especially, California were very desirable to the United States. The US population was growing, and people needed places to live, farm, and conduct business. California also offered valuable harbors on the Pacific coast. Many Americans had moved to these areas already, and they wanted the land to be ruled by the United States. Even many of the Mexican residents of these areas welcomed American settlers. New Mexico and California were the Mexican frontier, and their sparse populations were constantly under threat from surrounding American Indian peoples. The Mexicans saw American settlers as potential allies against the Indians.

Related to economics was the issue of slavery. Using slaves to work on farms was far less costly than hiring help, and the practice was common in the southern United States. Many farmers in Texas and across the Southwest wanted to use slave labor, but the practice was outlawed in Mexico. In the United States, though controversy over slavery was growing, the practice was still permitted. For supporters of slavery in the western territories, becoming part of the United States was in their best interest.

Although Congress overwhelmingly approved a declaration of war against Mexico, not all Americans were on board. A number of people and groups were outspoken in their opposition to the conflict. The Whigs, a prominent political party, felt that the desire for the land was greedy and the declaration of war unconstitutional. Abolitionist groups worried that if the new territories were admitted to the Union as slave states, their struggle to end slavery wouldn't succeed. Abraham Lincoln, then a first-term Whig congressman from Illinois, argued that the war was unnecessary and unjustified. American author Henry David Thoreau was briefly jailed for failing to pay taxes, which he said was a protest against the war.

The Mexican-American War itself was brief, lasting just two years. It is often just touched upon in the study of American history. For both Mexico and the United States, however, the effects of the war last to this day.

## CHAPTER ONE

# THE STORY OF TEXAS

The story of the Mexican-American War begins with the history of Texas. In the eighteenth century, Texas was under Spanish control. Although the United States and Spain had some conflict over the borders between their territories, Spain had control of the area by 1819, confirmed by the Transcontinental (or Adams-Onís) Treaty. After Mexico gained its independence from Spain in 1821, the boundary was confirmed by a treaty with the United States.

## INVITING THE AMERICANS

Few Mexicans wanted to move to Texas, which was a remote and isolated region. The Mexican government was deeply in debt following the fight for independence, and it couldn't spare many resources for the northernmost part of the country. The Mexican government decided to allow Americans to settle in the area.

In 1821, just before Mexico became independent, an American named Moses Austin had received permission from the Spanish colonial government to move 300 families to an area of about 200,000 acres (81,000 hectares). His sudden death left the project to his son, Stephen Austin, who took over with zeal. He convinced the new Mexican government that these white Americans would increase the value of the land and be loyal to Mexico, paying taxes and even converting to Catholicism, the religion of Mexico. The Mexican authorities agreed, making Austin a government official for the area. In 1824, Mexico officially opened its borders to settlers from the United States. Thousands of people came to claim land—so many that, in 1830, Mexico banned further settlement by Americans.

A statue of Moses Austin stands outside City Hall in San Antonio, Texas. Austin was the first American to receive permission to start a settlement in Spanish Texas.

### The Settlers of Texas

While Stephen Austin tried to work with the Mexican government, many new settlers wanted little to do with Mexico and its culture. They refused to learn the Spanish language, did not change their religion, and avoided interactions with the few Mexicans in the area. Many of the settlers also refused to follow Mexican custom, particularly when it came to slavery. When Mexico officially outlawed slavery in 1829, most settlers ignored the law, much to Mexico's dismay. The settlers felt that they were still Americans, bound only by American law. Mexico had assumed that the Americans would assimilate to its culture, which was the spirit of the agreement to let them in, but it was not to be. Mexico began restricting immigration and eventually closed the border, but Americans continued to claim land. By the early 1830s, there were more than 24,000 white settlers in Texas, compared to only about 3,400 Mexicans.

## THE REPUBLIC OF TEXAS

In 1833, instability in Mexico led to a coup by Antonio López de Santa Anna, who took the presidency. The people of Texas were hopeful that Santa Anna would allow them some freedom, but he instead imprisoned Stephen

Austin for encouraging an uprising against the Mexican government. After two years, Austin returned to Texas to find that relations between the white settlers and Mexican troops had become tense, and occasionally violent. The settlers decided to take action.

Antonio López de Santa Anna led Mexican troops during the Texas war for independence (1835–1836). He later served as a general during the Mexican-American War.

Texans formed a provisional government in 1835, and on March 2, 1836, it issued a declaration of independence at Washington-on-the-Brazos. David G. Burnet was named temporary president of the new Republic of Texas. Sam Houston was appointed its military commander. Austin became commissioner to the United States with the mission of securing strategic aid and enlisting volunteers.

The most famous event in the Texas war for independence was the defense of the Alamo in San Antonio. The Alamo was a former chapel that had become a Mexican military outpost. In December 1835, a group of recently

## Declaration of Independence

Texans laid out their arguments against Mexican rule in the Texas Declaration of Independence. Although a committee of five was appointed to draft the document, historians generally consider George Childress to be the author, most likely with little help from the others. Fifty-nine representatives from different parts of Texas approved the declaration. In the document, Childress summed up the complaints about what Texans viewed as the denial of their rights, including the right to bear arms and freedom of religion. The force of the document's opposition to Mexican rule can be seen in the opening lines:

> *"When a government has ceased to protect the lives, liberty and property of the people, from whom its legitimate powers are derived, and for the advancement of whose happiness it was instituted, and so far from being a guarantee for the enjoyment of those inestimable and inalienable rights, becomes an instrument in the hands of evil rulers for their oppression."*

arrived Americans took over the building. Houston and other Texan leaders advised them to abandon the site, warning that it would be impossible to defend with the small number of troops available. Nevertheless, the group—estimated to consist of between 183 and 189 men, though there may have been more—held its ground. On February 23, 1836, a Mexican army commanded by General Santa Anna began a siege of the Alamo. The Mexicans outnumbered the Americans at least ten to one, and possibly thirty to one. After thirteen days of fighting, Santa Anna's troops took the Alamo, killing nearly every American, on March 6, 1836.

"Remember the Alamo" became a battle cry for Texan troops, but an even deadlier event took place weeks

Percy Morgan's painting *Battle of the Alamo* depicts the deadly fighting between Mexican troops and Texans. The battle lasted nearly two weeks before the Alamo fell to Mexico.

later in Goliad. On March 20, 1836, a force of some 330 American and Texan troops under Colonel James Fannin surrendered to a larger Mexican force after the Battle of Coleto Creek. Fannin surrendered with the understanding that his men would be treated as prisoners of war. Instead, Santa Anna ordered his troops to execute almost all of Fannin's men. The Goliad Massacre solidified support among Americans for the war against Mexico.

## THE TIDE TURNS

Victory for Texas finally came at the Battle of San Jacinto. On April 21, 1836, after several days of retreat,

After several bloody defeats, Texas was victorious in the Battle of San Jacinto. The Texans defeated a larger Mexican army and captured General Santa Anna.

General Houston got his chance to attack Santa Anna's troops. The Mexican general, confident that the Texan troops were too small in number to be a real threat, left his encampment vulnerable by failing to build fences or put more than a few guards on duty. Houston seized this opportunity, winning the twenty-minute battle and killing hundreds of Mexican troops. General Santa Anna was captured and agreed to allow Texas to become independent.

## CHAPTER TWO

# TEXAS STATEHOOD LEADS TO WAR

Texas would not remain a republic for long. Months after winning its independence, Texas voted in favor of joining the United States. Texans still feared Mexico's large army, and they knew they might not win another battle over their land. They also faced occasional attacks by Native Americans. Their small army, called the Texas Rangers, had to cover large distances. Government finances were shaky, and from 1836 to 1845 the public debt grew from $1 million to $8 million. Also, because most Texans had come from the United States, they wanted the rights and protection they had enjoyed as citizens.

## DIFFERING OPINIONS

Many Americans opposed Texan statehood, largely because of the slavery question. Adding another slaveholding state to the Union would tip the balance between slave states and free states in slavery's favor, and Northerners strongly objected. Andrew Jackson, the US president at the time of the Texas Revolution, supported the annexation of Texas but did not want to provoke Mexico into war. The next president, Martin Van Buren, opposed annexation because it would add to the country's slave territory. Van Buren's successor, President John Tyler, tried to annex Texas but initially failed to get approval from Congress. Meanwhile, Mexico warned the United States that it would consider annexation to be a declaration of war.

US president Martin Van Buren (1837–1841) refused to grant Texas statehood because it would increase the country's slave territory. Texas would finally join the Union in 1845.

When James K. Polk campaigned for the US presidency in 1844, he took a strong stand in favor of annexing Texas. He won the election. As Polk was about to begin his presidency, he supported

Tyler's second effort to bring about the annexation. This time Congress approved the measure, and Tyler signed it on March 1, 1845. Eventually, in December, Texas would be admitted to the Union as the twenty-eighth state.

The annexation heightened tensions between the United States and Mexico. The situation was worsened by a dispute over the border between the two countries. Texas claimed that its southwestern boundary extended to the Rio Grande. This was the boundary accepted by the United States at the time of annexation. Mexico claimed that the boundary was the Nueces River, which is 100 miles (160 kilometers) eastward. In August 1845, President Polk stationed American troops west of the Nueces, showing that the United States would protect Texas to the Rio Grande but attempting at the same time to avoid war.

Mexican president José Joaquín de Herrera refused to sell any territory to the United States after the US annexation of Texas. Nevertheless, he wanted to resolve the dispute through negotiation, not war.

Mexican president José Joaquín de Herrera

agreed to meet with a representative from the United States, John Slidell. He hoped that Slidell would offer to compensate Mexico for the loss of Texas. However, Slidell planned to negotiate the purchase of even more Mexican land. He was to offer $5 million for the New Mexico territory and $25 million for California. Under pressure from his political opponents and the Mexican public, Herrera refused to even hear the offer. He was forced from the presidency soon after.

## GOLD!

California is a long way from Texas, but it was a big factor in the Mexican-American War. The United States wanted California for several reasons. One, it was the ultimate goal of expansionists to control the land from coast to coast. Two, the United States was afraid that European nations, such as Britain and France, wanted California as well. A European presence on the continent would be a big threat to America's independence. Finally, California had excellent farmland and other natural resources. The California Gold Rush, in which tens of thousands of Americans sought their fortunes after the discovery of gold in California in the mid-1800s, confirmed the area's worth to America in dollars. Between 1848 and the end of the 1850s, $2 billion worth of gold was mined in California.

## POLK'S BOLD MOVE

After Mexico's refusal to meet with Slidell, Polk ordered General Zachary Taylor to advance his troops to the Rio Grande. This was a hostile move that was meant to provoke Mexico. The Mexican government sent troops across the river to attack on April 25, 1846, wounding or killing sixteen American soldiers. Polk used this incident to claim that Mexico had "invaded our territory and shed American blood on American soil" in an address to Congress, which approved a declaration of war against Mexico on May 13.

The first two major battles of the war actually took place before war was declared. The Battle of Palo Alto occurred on May 8. Mexican troops had crossed the Rio Grande to attack Fort Brown and to threaten General Taylor's supply center. Although the US troops were outnumbered, they had stronger, more accurate cannons, which turned out to be the key to their victory. The next day, the Mexicans were forced to retreat. Taylor's troops followed them and scored a second victory in the Battle of Resaca de la Palma. In these two defeats, the Mexicans suffered hundreds of casualties and lost many supplies. Shortly after, on May 18, the Americans were able to cross the Rio Grande and occupy the city of Matamoros.

BY THE PRESIDENT OF THE UNITED STATES OF AMERICA.

A PROCLAMATION.

Whereas the Congress of the United States, by virtue of the constitutional authority vested in them, have declared by their act, bearing date this day, that, "by the act of the Republic of Mexico, a state of war exists between that Government and the United States:"

Now, therefore, I, JAMES K. POLK, President of the United States of America, do hereby proclaim the same to all whom it may concern; and I do specially enjoin on all persons holding offices, civil or military, under the authority of the United States, that they be vigilant and zealous in discharging the duties respectively incident thereto: and I do moreover exhort all the good people of the United States, as they love their country, as they feel the wrongs which have forced them on the last resort of injured nations, and as they consult the best means, under the blessing of Divine Providence, of abridging its calamities, that they exert themselves in preserving order, in promoting concord, in maintaining the authority and the efficacy of the laws, and in supporting and invigorating all the measures which may be adopted by the constituted authorities for obtaining a speedy, a just, and an honorable peace.

In testimony whereof, I have hereunto set my hand, and caused the seal of the United States to be affixed to these presents. Done at the City of Washington the thirteenth day [L. S.] of May, one thousand eight hundred and forty-six, and of the independence of the United States the seventieth.

JAMES K. POLK.

*By the President:*
JAMES BUCHANAN,
*Secretary of State.*

President James K. Polk issued a proclamation announcing that Congress had declared war on Mexico on May 13, 1846.

While the United States maintained that Mexico began the war, the Mexicans saw things differently. From their point of view, the United States had sent troops to their land, and Mexico was merely taking a defensive position against invaders. Mexican president Mariano Paredes y Arrillaga had no choice but to engage in the combat that was happening within his borders. His message to the Mexican Congress on July 6, 1846, explained his position clearly: "The government, in the natural defense of the nation, will repel the aggression initiated and sustained by the United States of America against the Republic of Mexico, having invaded and committed hostilities in a number of the departments making up Mexican territory." Whether Paredes wanted it or not, his country was at war with its northern neighbor. He could not afford to go to war, but he also could not leave his nation open to invasion.

Mariano Paredes y Arrillaga was president of Mexico when the Mexican-American War began. Following early Mexican losses, he was overthrown by Santa Anna.

# CHAPTER THREE

# FIGHTING IN MEXICO

When war broke out, former Mexican president and general Antonio López de Santa Anna (the conqueror of the Texan forces at the Alamo in 1836) contacted Polk. The US president arranged for a ship to take Santa Anna from Cuba to Mexico for the purpose of working for peace. Instead of acting for peace, however, on his return, Santa Anna took charge of the Mexican forces.

The United States sent its army from the Rio Grande, under General Taylor, to invade the heart of Mexico. A second force, under Colonel Stephen Kearny, was to occupy New Mexico and California. In almost every battle, the American troops were victorious, though they were outnumbered by the Mexicans by about two to one.

## THE STRUGGLE FOR MONTERREY

The city of Monterrey, located 100 miles (160 km) south of the Rio Grande, was the site of an important early battle. General Taylor led approximately 6,600 US

Mexican general Pedro de Ampudia surrenders the city of Monterrey to General Zachary Taylor. President Polk was displeased with the terms of surrender accepted by Taylor.

troops as they approached the city on September 19, 1846. Mexican army scouts had informed their general, Pedro de Ampudia, that the Americans were approaching. The general had 5,000 men waiting for them.

A fortress called the Citadel guarded Monterrey. In an effort to overcome this obstacle, General Taylor divided his troops to attack the city from two sides. General William J. Worth led the western force, while the east was handled by Colonel John Garland. Worth's troops managed to capture forts on Federation and Independence Hills, giving him a good view of the city. Garland's troops had a more difficult time fighting their way into the city,

A lithograph by Currier & Ives from about 1847 depicts a scene from the Battle of Buena Vista.

though they pushed forward with aid from a force led by General William O. Butler.

The Americans forced Ampudia's troops into the center of the city. The Mexican forces held their ground for several days. On September 23, an American attack led to fierce house-to-house fighting in the streets. The Mexicans surrendered the next day. Ampudia gave up Monterrey in return for a chance for his men to leave the city peacefully, with their weapons, and an eight-week-long armistice. Taylor agreed to these terms, which angered President Polk. He felt that Taylor had missed a chance to end the war quickly.

### Outmanned, but Victorious

In many of the early battles of the Mexican-American War, US troops were outnumbered by Mexicans. In some cases, Mexico had two soldiers for every American fighter. Mexico also had the advantage of fighting on its own terrain. How, then, did the United States win the war?

The Americans had a number of advantages. Their government was more stable than Mexico's, which changed hands several times during the war. Furthermore, Mexico was in a lot of debt, as it was still paying for its fight for independence. The United States had a stronger economy. Finally, while Mexico's army was fairly inexperienced, the United States had both established and volunteer troops, as well as a powerful navy.

## BATTLE OF BUENA VISTA

Following the victory at Monterrey, many of Taylor's troops were sent to other posts. The general was left with five thousand inexperienced troops. After learning of Taylor's weakened forces, Mexican general Santa Anna gathered twenty thousand troops to confront them. Taylor, knowing he was vastly outnumbered, moved south to La Angostura, near Buena Vista, on February 21, 1847, and waited for the enemy. The Americans were stationed on a pass between two mountain ranges.

This lithograph depicting the Battle of Buena Vista was based on a drawing made during the battle by one of its participants—Major Joseph Horace Eaton, aide-de-camp to General Taylor.

Disease and freezing weather reduced Santa Anna's forces by 30 percent, but they forged ahead. Santa Anna demanded that Taylor surrender, but Taylor refused. On February 23, the Mexicans attacked on the eastern side of Taylor's stronghold, which was left exposed.

The United States lost many men that day. Taylor was forced to call up reserve troops, the Mississippi Rifles. With their help, the Americans were able to force the Mexican troops back. In a day of heavy fighting, the Americans suffered losses of about seven hundred men, while the Mexicans lost more than twice as many. In the night, Santa Anna called for retreat. Taylor did not bother to follow him. He knew that the Mexican troops were so weakened that they were no longer a threat.

# CHAPTER FOUR

# PATH TO VICTORY

A year after the war began, it was clear that an American victory was imminent. Despite moments of success during some battles, the Mexicans did not achieve any major victories. They were in a state of constant retreat. The United States, however, continued to push forward.

## ON TO VERACRUZ

Because of President Polk's disappointment in General Taylor's performance, he decided to turn over control of the war to another general, Winfield Scott. With newly arrived troops, combined with Taylor's men, Scott invaded the key port city of Veracruz on March 9, 1847. Veracruz, on the Gulf of Mexico, was known at the time as the most strongly guarded port in North America.

US forces under General Winfield Scott land at Veracruz on March 9, 1847. The siege that led to the capture of the crucial port city was a joint effort of the US Army and Navy.

The operation began when ten thousand American soldiers arrived at Collado Beach, south of Veracruz. They were aided by naval forces under the command of Commodore David E. Conner. Scott's troops laid siege to Veracruz, trapping the Mexican troops in the city. The Mexicans could not communicate with Mexico City, nor could they receive supplies. The Americans spent days digging trenches around the city.

On March 22, General Scott demanded that the Mexican commander, General Juan Morales, surrender the city. Despite being outnumbered and surrounded,

General Winfield Scott took command of the US Army after the Battle of Monterrey. He captured Veracruz and went on to lead the troops in a series of brilliant victories in the late stages of the war.

Morales refused. Then Scott's troops and the navy began bombarding the city. General Morales handed control over to General Juan Landero, who surrendered on March 29. The United States now had an excellent port for receiving supplies and troops to continue its invasion of Mexico.

## DECISIVE ACTION AT CHAPULTEPEC

The spring and summer of 1847 were marked by a series of American victories, including the battles of

### SILENT KILLERS

Gunfire and cannons were not the only things American soldiers feared. Ultimately, infection and disease took many more US lives than combat did. At least 10,000 US soldiers died of illness, while only about 1,500 were killed in action or died of battle wounds. Poor sanitation helped spread illness, with volunteers—who were less educated about sanitary practices than regular troops were—dying in greater numbers than the regulars. Yellow fever was most common, but other diseases—such as measles, mumps, and smallpox—took their toll, too.

Cerro Gordo, Contreras, and Churubusco. US forces were moving west with a clear goal: to capture the capital, Mexico City.

Although the United States had lost many troops, the Mexicans had lost even more. After the Battle of Churubusco, General Scott offered an armistice to General Santa Anna. He hoped that Mexico would agree to a peaceful surrender. Santa Anna accepted the armistice, but he used the break from fighting to reinforce Mexico City's defenses.

In the Battle of Cerro Gordo, General Scott's force of 8,500 men met a Mexican force of 12,000 men under General Santa Anna. The Mexicans suffered about 1,130 casualties and had about 3,000 soldiers taken prisoner. The American loss was 431, including 63 dead.

Scott decided to move forward. The last obstacle on his path to Mexico City was Chapultepec, a rocky hill topped by a fortress. At the time, Chapultepec was being used as a military training school. It was also one of Mexico's landmark buildings and thus very meaningful to the people of Mexico. It was defended by about 5,000 soldiers, including cadets from the military school.

The Americans began their assault by bombarding the fort on September 12, 1847. Then they attacked on two fronts. General Gideon Pillow took the eastern

*Attack on the Castle Chapultepec* by Nathaniel Currier depicts the final battle before US troops entered Mexico City. General Scott's forces captured the fortress after facing the Mexicans in hand-to-hand combat.

position, while General John Quitman came up from the south. On September 13, the two forces climbed over the walls of the fort. The defenders resisted in fierce hand-to-hand combat, but the Americans prevailed within a few hours. Several Mexican cadets were killed, one of them, it is said, by leaping from the castle walls, holding the flag to keep it from being captured. These cadets are known in Mexican history as Los Niños Héroes—"Child Heroes." Altogether, the Mexicans lost 2,000 soldiers in the battle; the United States lost fewer than 500.

A mural on the ceiling of Chapultepec Castle honors Los Niños Héroes, the "Child Heroes" of the battle at the fortress. The mural was painted by Gabriel Flores García.

## TAKING MEXICO CITY

The Mexican army was forced to retreat to Mexico City to make its last stand. American troops followed them. Mexican citizens joined the fight, shooting at the US troops from the rooftops. With his army weakened, and seeing no way out, Santa Anna was forced to admit defeat. He left Mexico City with his remaining soldiers. The next day—September 14, 1847—a group of Mexican officials surrendered the city to the United States.

## CHAPTER FIVE

# WHEN THE DUST SETTLED

The fighting was over, but the official end of the war was still several months away. The peace terms still had to be negotiated. The peace treaty would have profound and lasting consequences for both Mexico and the United States.

## TREATY OF GUADALUPE-HIDALGO

President Polk sent Nicholas Trist, chief clerk in the State Department, to negotiate a peace treaty. The talks were long delayed, however, as Mexico worked to form a government capable of negotiations. Polk grew impatient and told Trist to return home. Trist disobeyed the president's order and went forward with the negotiations.

Nicholas Trist was empowered by President Polk to negotiate the terms of peace with Mexico. When Polk ordered Trist to stop the negotiations and return home, Trist boldly refused.

Trist and Mexico's representatives came to a final agreement on February 2, 1848. It was called the Treaty of Guadalupe-Hidalgo, after the town in which it was signed. By the terms of the treaty, Mexico gave up its claim to Texas and accepted the Rio Grande as its boundary. The treaty gave the United States more than 525,000 square miles (1,360,000 square km) of Mexican land. This land now includes all or parts of the states of California, New Mexico, Nevada, Utah, Arizona, Wyoming, Texas, and Colorado. The treaty allowed Mexico to retain the Baja Peninsula, south of California. Mexico received $15 million for the land and was relieved of $3 million in claims that US citizens had made against Mexico.

## THE WAR'S LEGACY

Mexico gained nothing from the war. The money paid to Mexico by the United States was not enough to repair all of the damage done. Families were destroyed, and many people lost their land. The questionable character of the American claims to Mexican lands contributed a heritage of ill will to the troubled relations between Mexico and the United States. In addition, for many Mexicans the

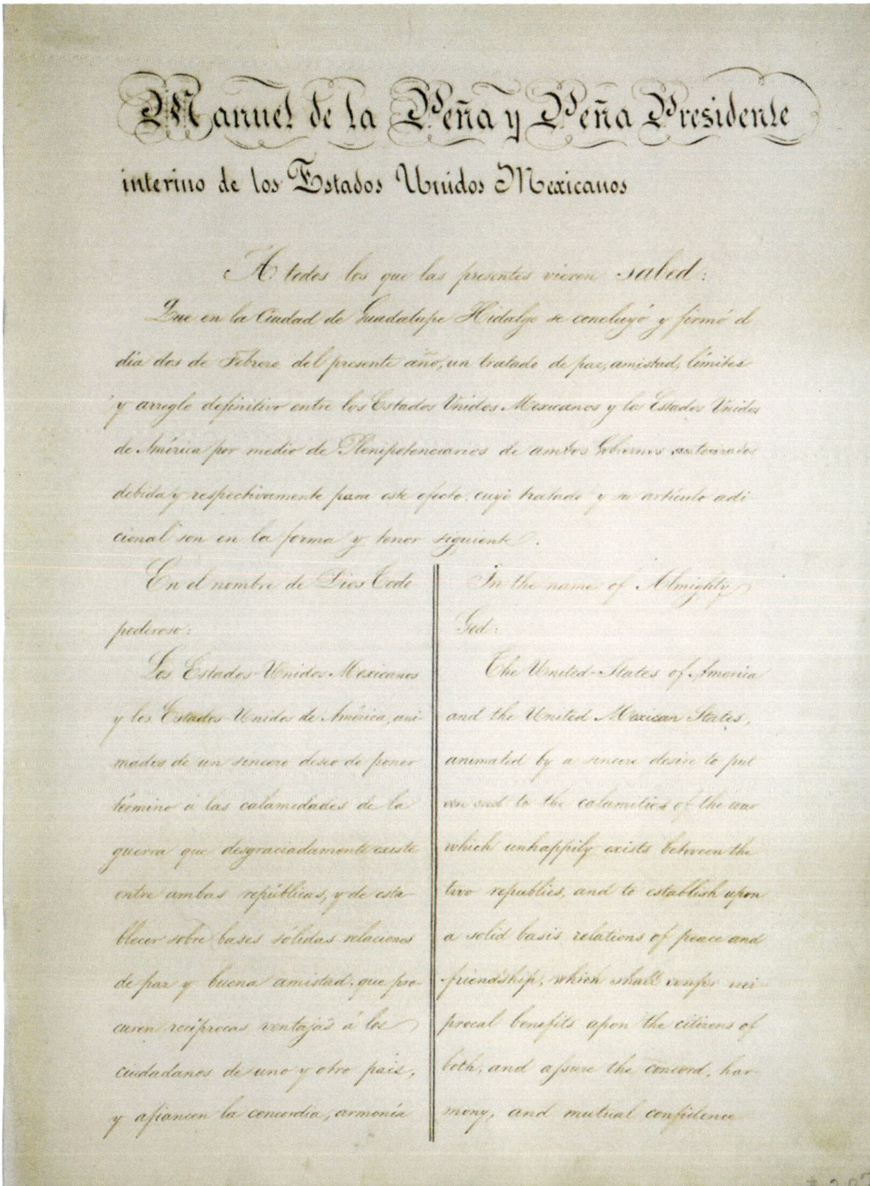

Manuel de la Peña y Peña Presidente interino de los Estados Unidos Mexicanos

A todos los que las presentes vieren sabed:

Que en la Ciudad de Guadalupe Hidalgo se concluyó y firmó el día dos de Febrero del presente año, un tratado de paz, amistad, límites y arreglo definitivo entre los Estados Unidos Mexicanos y los Estados Unidos de América por medio de Plenipotenciarios de ambos Gobiernos autorizados debida y respectivamente para este efecto, cuyo tratado y su artículo adicional son en la forma y tenor siguiente:

En el nombre de Dios Todo poderoso:

Los Estados Unidos Mexicanos y los Estados Unidos de América, animados de un sincero deseo de poner término á las calamidades de la guerra que desgraciadamente existe entre ambas repúblicas, y de establecer sobre bases sólidas relaciones de paz y buena amistad, que procuren recíprocas ventajas á los ciudadanos de uno y otro país, y afiancen la concordia, armonía

In the name of Almighty God:

The United States of America and the United Mexican States, animated by a sincere desire to put an end to the calamities of the war which unhappily exists between the two republics, and to establish upon a solid basis relations of peace and friendship, which shall confer reciprocal benefits upon the citizens of both, and assure the concord, harmony, and mutual confidence

The Treaty of Guadalupe-Hidalgo gave the United States a vast territory that had been Mexican land. In return, Mexico received some financial compensation.

loss of so much territory damaged their feelings of national pride.

The United States acquired vast mineral wealth, especially gold, and a door to the Pacific Ocean and to East Asia. This led to the famed California Gold Rush, in which people moved west to seek their fortunes. The vast new territory attracted many Americans who were looking to start a new life.

## The Cost of War

War is very expensive for both the winners and the losers. Soldiers must be paid. Weapons and ammunition must be manufactured or purchased. Food and clothing must be delivered. Medical supplies are crucial, as are means of transportation—at the time of the Mexican-American War, horses, wagons, and boats. The host of the war also has the cost of rebuilding forts, bridges, roads, towns, and villages. It is estimated that the United States spent $75 million on the Mexican-American War. In today's dollars, that's about $2.3 billion.

The greater cost of war is the loss of human life. In total, the United States lost more than 11,000 soldiers during the war, from battle wounds or disease. Mexico's casualties numbered around 25,000. That number represents both military and civilian losses.

The additional territory raised again the burning question of slavery in the United States. The Missouri Compromise of 1820 had banned slavery in any new states north of Missouri's southern border. This was an effort to satisfy both the North and the South. However, the debate reignited over the status of slavery in the newly acquired lands.

Soon after the Mexican-American War began in 1846, Congressman David Wilmot of Pennsylvania proposed an amendment to a bill that would have banned slavery in any territory acquired from

The United States gained vast gold deposits when it acquired California from Mexico. This illustration shows miners digging for gold in California in the early 1850s, during the famous Gold Rush.

Congressman David Wilmot tried to ban slavery from the new territory acquired from Mexico, but he was unsuccessful. Slavery would remain a heated issue until the Civil War.

Mexico. The Wilmot Proviso did not pass, but it raised tensions between North and South. The slavery question was eventually settled by the Compromise of 1850, but again only temporarily. Just over a decade later, the issue would lead to civil war.

# GLOSSARY

**abolitionist** A person who wanted to abolish, or end, slavery in the 1700s and 1800s.

**acquire** To come into possession or control of.

**annex** To incorporate a territory within the domain of a country.

**armistice** A pause in fighting brought about by agreement between the two sides.

**assimilate** To absorb into the culture of another group.

**bombard** To attack with weapons that shoot, such as cannons.

**cadet** A person training for the military.

**casualty** A death or injury due to war.

**compensate** To make an appropriate payment to, typically to make up for something.

**conflict** An extended struggle; a fight or battle.

**coup** The overthrow of an existing government.

**economic** Having to do with money.

**hostile** Showing opposition; unfriendly.

**imminent** About to happen.

**negotiation** Discussion meant to come to an agreement.

**occupy** To take or hold possession or control of.

**provisional** Temporary.

**reinforce** To make stronger.

**retain** To keep.

**retreat** To move back from an enemy.

**sanitation** Processes that promote cleanliness and prevent the spread of germs (such as the removal of sewage and trash).

**siege** A military blockade of a city or fortified place to force it to surrender.

**unjustified** Not deserved or appropriate.

# FOR FURTHER READING

Behnke, Alison. *A Timeline History of the Mexican-American War.* Minneapolis, MN: Lerner Publications, 2015.

Carey, Charles W. *The Mexican-American War.* New York, NY: Enslow Publishing, 2017.

DiConsiglio, John. *The Mexican-American War.* Chicago, IL: Heinemann, 2012.

Gaddi, Rosalie. *The U.S.-Mexican War and Its Impact on the United States.* New York, NY: PowerKids Press, 2016.

Peppas, Lynn. *Why Stephen F. Austin Matters to Texas.* New York, NY: PowerKids Press, 2013.

Shoup, Kate. *Texas and the Mexican War.* New York, NY: Cavendish Square Publishing, 2016.

Stanley, Joseph. *The Expansion of the United States: Florida, Alaska, Gadsden Purchase, and Mexican Cession.* New York, NY: PowerKids Press, 2017.

Walker, Paul Robert. *Remember the Alamo: Texians, Tejanos, and Mexicans Tell Their Stories.* Washington, DC: National Geographic, 2015.

# WEBSITES

Because of the changing nature of internet links, Rosen Publishing has developed an online list of websites related to the subject of this book. This site is updated regularly. Please use this link to access this list:

http://www.rosenlinks.com/WEST/War

# INDEX

## A



## B



## C



## F



## G



## H



## J



## M

## N



## O



## P



## R



## S



## T



## V



## W